# DISNEY

# MARY POPPINS RETURNS

## The Magic of Mary Poppins

By Bonnie Steele

Screenplay by David Magee

Based on the series of books by P. L. Travers

Houghton Mifflin Harcourt

Boston   New York

Mary Poppins is a no-nonsense nanny who is practically perfect in every way. She even has a knack for making the impossible possible.

She first meets John, Annabel, and Georgie Banks when she magically floats down from the clouds on the tail of Georgie's kite.

With her parrot umbrella and carpetbag in hand, Mary Poppins has returned to take care of the next generation of Banks children.

Michael and Jane Banks are thrilled to see their former nanny, who appears not to have aged since they last saw her. She says she will stay until the door opens. Which door does she mean?

John and Annabel don't think they need a nanny. They quickly change their minds, however, when Mary Poppins turns bath time into an extraordinary adventure.

Whenever the children are feeling lost or sad, Mary Poppins offers comfort and a kind smile. How does she always know the right things to do and say?

Mary Poppins may seem prim and proper, but she loves to sing and entertain. She finds an element of fun in even the most everyday tasks.

And her friends are just as wonderful as she is, especially Jack the lamplighter.

With a little bit of magic, Mary Poppins transports the children and their friend Jack to the fantastic world inside their mother's favorite china bowl.

Mary Poppins is greeted like a long-lost friend by penguins, a canine coachman, and other colorful characters.

The magic of Mary Poppins is that she's always there when needed—whether she's helping save the Bankses' house or making sure the spring fair is one to be remembered!

When joy and wonder are back in the Bankses' lives, Mary Poppins knows it is time for her to go. As the front door blows open at 17 Cherry Tree Lane, she floats off into the sky again.